JADV-PIC LAN
The stamp collector /

D0606721

VE JUN 2013
PR NOV 2015

OF JUN 2017

KR OCT 2020

The Stamp Collector

Jennifer Lanthier

Illustrations by
François Thisdale

Fitzhenry & Whiteside

Text copyright © 2012 Jennifer Lanthier
Illustrations copyright © 2012 François Thisdale

Published in Canada by Fitzhenry & Whiteside, 195 Allstate Parkway, Markham, Ontario L3R 4T8
Published in the United States by Fitzhenry & Whiteside, 311 Washington Street, Brighton, Massachusetts 02135

All rights reserved. No part of this book may be reproduced in any manner without the express written consent of the publisher, except in the case of brief excerpts in critical reviews and articles. All inquiries should be addressed to Fitzhenry & Whiteside Limited, 195 Allstate Parkway, Markham, Ontario L3R 4T8.

www.fitzhenry.ca   godwit@fitzhenry.ca
10 9 8 7 6 5 4 3 2 1
Library and Archives Canada Cataloguing in Publication
Lanthier, Jennifer
The stamp collector / Jennifer Lanthier ; illustrations
by François Thisdale.
ISBN 978-1-55455-218-4
I. Thisdale, François, 1964- II. Title.
PS8623.A69877S73 2012   jC813'.6   C2012-904071-1
Publisher Cataloging-in-Publication Data (U.S)
Lanthier, Jennifer
The stamp collector / Jennifer Lanthier ; illustrations by François Thisdale.
[32] p. : cm.

Summary: This tale of a city boy who loves stamps and a country boy who loves stories explores issues such as social justice, freedom of expression, human rights and political oppression.

ISBN: 978-1-55455-218-4 (pbk.)
1. Friendship— Juvenile fiction. I. Thisdale, François. II. Title.
[Fic] dc23   PZ7.L3684St 2012
Fitzhenry & Whiteside acknowledges with thanks the Canada Council for the Arts, and the Ontario Arts Council for their support of our publishing program. We acknowledge the financial support of the Government of Canada through the Canada Book Fund (CBF) for our publishing activities.

Canada Council   Conseil des Arts
for the Arts   du Canada

ONTARIO ARTS COUNCIL
CONSEIL DES ARTS DE L'ONTARIO

Design by CommTech Unlimited
Printed in Canada by Friesens

MIX
Paper from
responsible sources
FSC® C016245
www.fsc.org

Foreword

Stories: Words and pictures that connect human beings through time and space, whether across centuries and continents, or a room in the here and now. These bonds, as delicate as squiggles on paper, are a glue sufficiently strong to terrify the most powerful forces in the world.

The Stamp Collector is an elegantly crafted picture book for children and adults. A boy who loves books and a boy who loves stamps grow into men separated by background, position, and cell bars; yet, at the end of a lifetime, these barriers are nothing when set beside the power of Story to connect and transform their lives.

We are told that stories are frills, that they are nothing next to the might of systems, numbers, and bureaucracies. *The Stamp Collector* reminds us that this is a lie. Stories light up our hearts and imaginations. They let us see ourselves in the Other and the Other in ourselves, and in that moment the world is changed forever. As John the Evangelist wrote, in another context: "The light shines in the darkness, and the darkness has never been able to put it out."

Allan Stratton
author of *Chanda's Secrets*

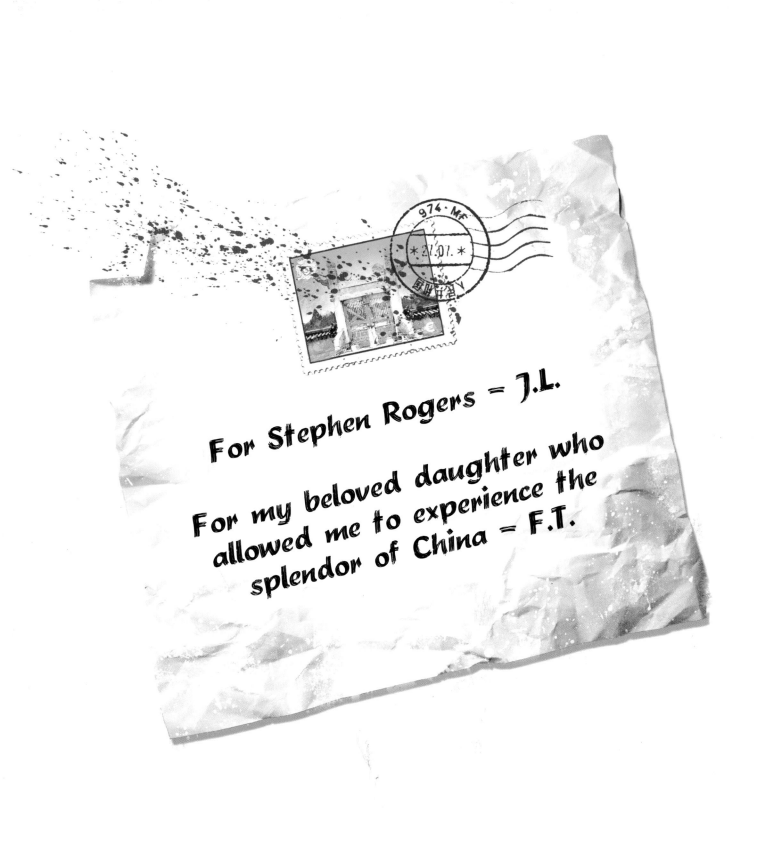

For Stephen Rogers = J.L.

For my beloved daughter who
allowed me to experience the
splendor of China = F.T.

This is the story of not long ago and not far away.
It is the story of a boy who loves stamps and a boy who loves words.
This is the story of a life that is lost.
And found.

登机口于起飞前10分钟关闭

A city boy living in the shadow of a grey prison finds a scrap of paper on the street.
It is empty, stained, and torn. Forgotten.
There is nothing remarkable about this envelope.
Except its stamp.

The boy takes it home to show his grandfather.
"It is not rare or precious," the grandfather says.
He holds a magnifying glass over the emerald-green stamp.
"But it is beautiful."

Not far from the prison there is a moss-green village and a country boy who loves words.
He reads every book in his home but it is not enough. The country boy craves stories.
He devours every poem and fable in his school and his library. Still he hungers.
For stories.

In the field, the children call to the boy to put down his book and join their game.
He cannot hear—he is tumbling through time and racing across the stars.
Soon he begins to find stories all around him. He learns to capture them.
He writes.

As the city boy tucks the stamp under his pillow he knows it is precious.
The stamp has traveled far—farther than the boy could imagine.
The boy has never dreamed of far-off places.
Until now.

In his dreams, the stamp is a kite, a paper jewel from the crown of a wise old king.
It holds a secret message; it is a clue to buried treasure.
The stamp is the key to another world—one that is new and full of adventure.
And stories.

But the smoke-filled city is hard and the boy is poor.
Dreams do not buy bread.
It is his duty to help his family,
to grow big and strong, to find work.
As soon as he is old enough, the city boy leaves school.
He takes a job as a prison guard.

But he keeps the stamp.

The country boy sees the crops fail and the stream run black.
Stories do not buy bread.
As soon as he is old enough, the country boy leaves school.
He goes to work in a factory.
But deep inside him, a story grows and grows,
filling his soul until he almost bursts.

He writes.

He writes of a land that is choking and dying, until the children bring it back to life.
His story brings joy and hope to the villagers. But it brings fear to others.
The factory owners complain to the grey men who run the village:
Make him stop.

While the village sleeps, men in uniforms arrest the writer and take him away.
He is not allowed to say goodbye to his parents or friends. Not allowed to speak.
The grey men say *words are dangerous.* They send the writer to prison.
No more stories.

The prison is cold and has many rules: no talking, no friendship, no laughter.
The boy who became a guard and the boy who became a writer are lonely.
They do not know that the writer's story is spreading across the land.
Bringing hope.

Years pass. One day, a letter arrives for the writer, but he is not allowed to see it.
The guard wonders why a letter would come from so far away. But he does not ask.
He must not break the rules. The guard places the letter in a file to be forgotten.
But he saves the stamp.

The letter is followed by another and then another. The file grows thick.
The stamps are so beautiful—bright and colorful, large and small.
They are like seeds blown by powerful winds from all corners of the world.
Like wishes.

One night the guard dreams that all his new stamps are escaping.
He tries to snatch them back but they fly away, back to their far-off countries.
When he awakes, he trembles with relief to find the stamps are still in their box.
Not free.

The next day, the guard opens the file. He reads the letters.
Some are written in his language; many use alphabets he has never seen.
Some are in crayon, others in ink. Some have drawings. Some are from old people.
Most are from children.

In his cell, the writer sits, imagining the visitors he is not allowed to see. He is hungry and sick.
The guard appears. He sees the writer shiver.
The guard hesitates then slides something small and bright between the bars.
A stamp.

At first the writer and the guard do not speak. They must not break the rules.
But the next day the guard brings another stamp. Then another. The writer smiles.
Every stamp tells a story without words. The writer knows he is not alone now.
Not forgotten.

But the prison is a hard, grey place; the writer is now much older than his years.
He begins to cough and the sound pierces the guard's heart with dread.
Now, instead of a stamp, the guard brings a letter. And another, and another.
The writer reads.

The letters tell of how his story was passed, from reader to reader, all around the world.
Adults write of the joy his story brought them, and about change and hope.
Children send their own stories and songs and poems. Everyone begs for one more story.
Just one more.

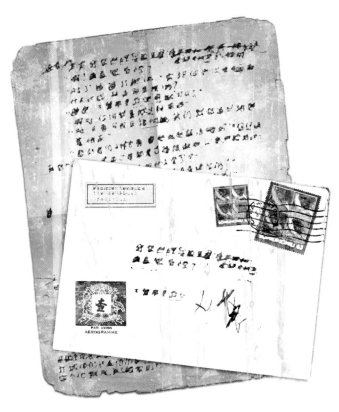

The guard sees the letters tremble in the writer's hands.
He hears the cough.
He thinks about his job, his parents, and his safe life.
And about the prison rules.
The guard doesn't believe he is brave enough
or strong enough.
But he says to the writer:
"Tell me."

Each day, the writer grows weaker.
Yet, in whispers, he tells the guard a new story.
And the story fills the guard's soul until he wonders
if he will burst.
He marvels at the words that soar and swoop and
thrill and break his heart.
"Again," he pleads. "Again."

The guard's grandfather once told him of a beautiful library far, far away.
A place for people who love words and stories. A place for writers.
But the writer's cough grows stronger. The guard knows he will never be free.
It is too late.

On a cold grey dawn in November, the guard waits by the writer's side.
At first neither speaks—the prison doctor is watching.
But the guard holds the writer's hand until the end.
He whispers, "Goodbye, Friend."

Alone, the guard sits and thinks about the writer and the prison and the grey men.
The guard wonders if he is truly brave enough or strong enough.
Then he hugs his mother and father goodbye; he does not tell them his plans.
Too dangerous.

The road is long and lonely, and the guard is hungry and tired by journey's end.
But the library is warm and safe and full of people who love words and stories.
The guard takes a small, emerald-green stamp from his pocket. He hesitates.
Then he writes:

This is the story of not long ago and not far away.

It is the story of a boy who loved stamps

And a boy who loved words.

This is the story of a life that was lost

And found.

Freedom to Write, Freedom to Read

This story was inspired by two writers: Nurmuhemmet Yasin and Jiang Weiping.

Jiang Weiping is a journalist who spent six years in a Chinese prison for exposing government corruption. Nurmuhemmet Yasin is a writer serving ten years in a Chinese prison for writing a short story called "The Wild Pigeon."

They are two of the countless writers who have been imprisoned all over the world.

These writers are not in jails or work camps because they committed theft or violence or fraud. They're in prison because of something they wrote.

Some countries have laws that protect freedom of speech or expression. Many do not. In some countries, the most dangerous thing you could do might be to write a poem, a story, or an essay. Anything that could offend a person with power is risky. It doesn't matter if the story is fiction or non-fiction. And it doesn't have to be published in a book or newspaper or magazine—you could be jailed and your family could be threatened for something you wrote online.

In some countries, when a piece of writing catches the eye of a government official—perhaps because it wins a literary award or brings attention to a problem the government doesn't want discussed—the writer is put on trial. The trial is often held in secret and the writer is not allowed to speak with a lawyer. When the trial ends, the writing is banned and the writer sent to a prison or work camp, sometimes for many years. Conditions there are often harsh, and prisoners may not receive proper nutrition or medical care.

Sometimes writers are tortured or killed before anyone even knows they have been imprisoned.

A group of writers called PEN International set up its first Writers in Prison Committee in 1960. Since then, advocates from all over the world have tried to help imprisoned writers, mostly by writing letters. Advocates write to governments, asking for the writer's release. And they write to prisoners and their families, to reassure them that they are not forgotten.

Today, PEN is joined by groups such as the Committee to Protect Journalists and Reporters Without Borders. Sometimes all they can do is persuade government or prison officials to treat the writer less harshly while he or she is in jail. But sometimes they succeed in having writers and reporters released early from their prison sentences.

Nurmuhemmet Yasin is still in prison; nobody is allowed to see him. But Jiang Weiping is free. Thanks to PEN Canada, he now lives with his family in Toronto.

It is Jiang Weiping who first told me of the importance of stamps.

A portion of the proceeds from this book will support PEN Canada in its efforts to bring hope to writers in prisons around the world.

= Jennifer Lanthier

3 3132 03448 1707
OKANAGAN REGIONAL LIBRARY